Cedar Cottage

Leslee Holmes

Published by New Generation Publishing in 2020

Copyright © Leslee Holmes 2020

First Edition

The author asserts the moral right under the Copyright, Designs and Patents Act 1988 to be identified as the author of this work.

All Rights reserved. No part of this publication may be reproduced, stored in a retrieval system or transmitted, in any form or by any means without the prior consent of the author, nor be otherwise circulated in any form of binding or cover other than that which it is published and without a similar condition being imposed on the subsequent purchaser.

ISBN

Paperback	978-1-80031-792-5
Hardback	978-1-80031-791-8

www.newgeneration-publishing.com

New Generation Publishing

Cedar Cottage

On the B9696 Stambridge road between Paglesham and Rochford is the village of Stambridge, a semi-rural village in Essex, a village dating back to the Domesday Book, a village consisting of a pub (The Oak), the obligatory church (St Mary's) and approximately 175 dwellings, one of which is Cedar Cottage, a 4 bedroom detached brick building built in the mid-1800s standing proudly next to Stambridge road.

Next to Cedar Cottage, to its left, is a 3 bedroom bungalow called Rowbottoms owned by Jack Rowbottom, a widower who was as old as the village. To the right of his cottage was another detached 3 bedroom house, then a row of houses dating back to the 18th century originally used for the workers who worked for Edwin Charles the land owner.

My name is Lee Carpenter, 50, a body of Adonis (yeah, I wish). I bought the house back in 2006 and from the moment we – that's my wife Ann, 48, and two kids Anthony, 15, and Leanne, 13, moved in I felt something was not quite right.

It was in the spring of 2006, we just got the keys to Cedar Cottage and we were very excited.

'We're moving, we're moving,' sang Leanne.

'Shut up,' barked Anthony.

'Anthony, don't talk to your sister like that,' scolded Ann. 'Now kids I said, keep a look out for our new house, it should be on the right next to some trees.'

As we turned the bend we saw it.

'There it is,' shouted Leanne.

'Shut up,' said Anthony again.

'What did I say?' said Ann to Anthony again, sharply.

As we pulled in to the drive I noticed a few things needed repairing which I hadn't noticed when we viewed it previously.

'You will have to do them before we start decorating the inside' said Ann.

I thought *yeah, master of the obvious*, not that I would have said that to her face of course. We stopped the car and got out, put the key in the door lock and went inside the house. There was a strange smell about the place it was like a combination of burnt charcoal and rotten fish; it was putrid to say the least.

'Jesus,' said Ann, a part-time Catholic who attended mass nearly every Sunday with her parents.

'Charming,' I said.

'No,' said Ann, 'it stinks. I don't remember it smelling this awful when we viewed it.'

'I'll open the windows,' I said. As I walked in to the front room I noticed on the bare floor there was a sort of lump. It wasn't a big lump, more like a well, little lump, which you wouldn't have noticed if had been carpeted. I didn't take any notice of it and carried on doing what I was doing, which was nothing really, just waiting for the furniture to turn up.

It was about six months later, we had settled in and done all the chores that needed doing and that it was then we noticed strange things beginning to happen. We discovered Leanne had an invisible friend; we would hear her whispering and laughing with it. When we entered the room she would be asleep. I asked her who was she talking to the next day and she answered 'no one, Dad, I was asleep.'

'Yes you did,' snapped Anthony, 'you were talking to that cat.'

'A cat,' I said surprisingly.

'Yes,' said Anthony, 'that's what she kept calling it.'

I just sighed, had words with them both and didn't think any more about it. It was in early November, I remember it was bloody freezing, and I got up for work at

05.30. The windows in the front room were open, not on the jar but wide open. I remember checking them before I went to bed and they were both locked shut. The first thing I thought was that we had been burgled but nothing had been taken. I thought, *strange, both of the windows being open wide like that* as I left for work. I didn't say anything to Ann as I didn't want to worry her and nothing had been taken. From that day other things started happening like things disappearing and re-appearing in different places. On one occasion I couldn't sleep so I decided to get up and go downstairs to make a cup of tea. Halfway down the stairs I heard some noises from the front room, strange murmuring noises as if someone was talking and that smell returned. I continued down the stairs into the living room making as much noise as I dare not to wake the kids only to find the room empty.

It was the same November, November 28th to be precise, when I received a phone call from Joan, Mum's friend.

'Your mum's been taken into hospital, she fell over.'

'Oh god is she alright?' I asked.

'It was a bit of a bad fall,' she answered.

'Where is she?'

'Colchester General, Gainsborough Wing, Birch ward,' she replied.

'OK,' I said, 'we are on our way.'

'What's happened?' asked Ann as I replaced the handset.

'Mum's fallen over and is in hospital.'

'Right I'll get my mum and dad to come and sit with the kids,' said Ann.

'look after Leanne Anthony', Ann said,

'why' he answered,

'something happened to nanny Liz, she's fallen over and is in hospital we are going to see her' said Ann, 'other nan and grandad are on their way over listen out for them' I said to him, ‘ok answered Anthony give her my love’ , ‘will do’ said Ann following me through the front door,

We arrived at the ward and mum was just lying there.

‘Hi, Mum, what happened?’

‘I was walking back from the shops with Joan when I tripped up that kerb outside the house and fell over,’ she said, ‘and they want to keep me in for observation and tests.’

‘Well, it’s for the best, Mum,’ I said.

We stayed as long as we could then left for home. We went back the next morning.

‘She’s OK. We can’t see anything untoward,’ said the doctor. ‘She’s OK to go home but she can’t stay on her own though, I’m afraid, not for a good few weeks. Is there anyone she can stay with?’

‘Yes, us,’ said Ann.

‘Thanks, love,’ I said, knowing they never really got on.

‘Liz, we are taking you home to get some clothes then you’re coming home with us for a couple of weeks,’ said Ann.

‘OK, that will be nice,’ Mum replied. ‘Thank you.’

I phoned Glen that afternoon to see if he was doing anything,

‘when’ he asked’,

‘now’ I said,

‘now why’s that’ replied Glen ,

‘mum’s had a fall and she’s coming home with us I need a hand to bring the bed down and sort out the dining room, she can’t make the stairs’,

‘oh sorry to hear that mate is she ok ‘ he asked,

‘a badly sprained ankle,

‘ouch ok mate I’ll see you soon came the reply’.

At about 7 o’clock that evening there was a knock on the door and standing there was Ann’s younger brother, Glen. Glen was a builder, 38, single, built like me, so nothing to write home about.

‘Hiya, sorry I haven’t been round.’

‘That’s OK,’ I said, ‘nice to see you after all this time.’

‘Had a lot on,’ he replied.

‘Where’s sis?’

‘Here,’ she said, advancing towards him and planting a kiss on his cheek.

’What’s happening?’ asked Glen.

‘Nothing much,’ I said. ‘As you know, Mum’s had an accident and we think we have a ghost.’

‘No, wicked. Have you seen it?’ joked Glen as he made his way into the kitchen to grab a beer out of the fridge. I explained to him what had been happening and he offered to sleep over.

‘I’ll take the spare room,’ he said.

We got the bed down the stairs from the bedroom into the dining room.

‘What are we doing with the table and chairs?’ Glen asked.

‘Stack the chairs over there in the corner and we can put the table in the front room’, I said ‘it’s only for a couple of weeks.’

‘Yeah, you’re hoping once she gets used to the company you will never get rid of her,’ said Glen.

‘Well, we will see. She’s still my mum,’ I said.

That night, Ann went to bed about 10o’clock. I sat up talking to Mum and glen about nothing particular and we all turned in about midnight.

‘Can you leave the passage light on just in case I need the loo?’ asked Mum.

‘OK,’ I said. ‘Good night mum, I’ll see you in morning. If you need anything give me a shout.’

‘I should be alright she replied, Good night Lee good night Glen’, good night Liz came a reply from the top of the stairs.

It was about 2.00 a.m. when we were woken up by a piercing scream.

‘What’s that?’ said Ann.

‘It’s Mum,’ I said, putting on my dressing gown as I ran out of the bedroom and down the stairs.

'What is it, Dad?' asked Leanne.

'Go back to bed, it's only Nan.' Said Ann

'What's wrong with Nanny'?

'Go back to bed now!' screamed Ann.

I hurried down the stairs, followed very closely by Glen and Ann.

'What is it, Mum?' I asked, turning her light on.

'What's wrong, Liz?' said Glen. She was sitting up, shaking whilst holding her sheet to her face.

'What happened?' said Ann, putting her arm around her shoulders. She pointed to the corner of the room.

'There,' she said.

'What?' I said.

'I don't know. It's gone now. It was a shadow, it moved from that corner,' pointing to the opposite side of the room, 'to there, to that corner.'

'What did it look like?' I asked.

'A bloody shadow!' she shouted.

'Tall? Short?' I asked.

'I don't know, it just moved. I don't want to stay in this room anymore, I want to go home.'

We sat up the rest of the night. I reported in sick next morning and had the next few days off work.

'I'll stay to the end of the week,' said Glen,

'Thanks,' I said.

Glen swapped rooms with Mum. She felt more comfortable upstairs and nothing happened for the rest of that week. We managed to decorate the bathroom and replace the bathroom suite with a new one, so it wasn't a complete waste of time Glen being there,

'I'll have to go tomorrow' said Glen 'as I've just picked up a job in Ipswich,'

'OK,' I said, 'thanks, mate.'

It was a Friday night, a week later, Glen had gone on his job, Ann was in bed watching TV, the kids were in bed asleep, Mum was knitting in her room, I had a bath.

This is nice, I thought as I soaked. It was about fifteen minutes later when I noticed the door handle move. 'I'm in here!' I shouted, there was no reply. The door handle moved yet again, up and down, up and down, gradually getting faster and faster. Then there was a thumping noise against the door. I thought *what the hell?* I clambered out of the bath, grabbing the moving door handle, only for it to stop. I opened the door. There was nobody there. I put a towel around me and checked the kids, Mum, then Ann. They were all asleep.

'What is it?' Ann said, rousing.

'Nothing, sweetheart, go back to sleep.' I said,

It was a week later that we took mum home to her flat and with a sigh of relief she said 'It's good to be home' as she hobbled through the door.

As I left her she took my arm and said 'Lee, sell that house. Nothing is right with it, get out as quickly as you can.'

I said 'There's nothing wrong with the house, Mum. Phone me if you need anything, bye.'

With that she closed the door behind me. Although I am not a religious person and I would never knock any religion, my wife is (when it suits her), and she suggested asking her priest, Father Patrick to come and bless the house.

After about two weeks he decided to turn up to do the blessing carrying a big black bag in hand.

'I wouldn't normally do this for outsiders,' he said in the loud, obnoxious voice he had, having a dig at me for not attending his bloody services, 'but seeing as Ann is a valued customer and a friend I will do this just the once,' turning and smiling at Ann.

You prat, I thought to myself.

'Right, I'm off,' said Ann.

'Anywhere nice?' said Father Patrick.

'Ooh anywhere nice?' I said under my breath, sarcastically.

'Only shopping, it's all I ever seem to do,' she said, laughing as she disappeared through the front door.

'Have a nice time!' he shouted.

'Do you want a cup of tea, Pat?' I said.

'No thanks,' he replied as he opened his big black bag to reveal a rather large-looking cross, a bible, along with a few other odds and sods.

'Anything else? Coffee? A beer?' I asked.

'No really, I'm fine,' he said,

'Um, where are the children?' he asked.

'At school,' I said. 'Why?'

'Good, so there is no one in the house at the moment?' he enquired.

'Only us why I said,

'nothing nothing' he replied

'Ok then I'll see you later I am only out in the garden if you want anything' I said inquisitively,

'Ok replied the priest',

I went back outside into the garden to carry on mowing my lawn leaving father Patrick in the kitchen,

'Right' said the priest placing his orarium or stole as its commonly known around his neck, 'let's get this done' he mumbled under his breath, leaving the kitchen with bible in one hand and the cross in the other he entered the lounge then the dining room blessing each room as he went, ascending the stairs up through the mezzanine floor he reached the landing,

In front of him were the 4 bedrooms and bathroom, He entered leanness room first, blessing the room as he went in. Behind a chair in the corner of the room he saw something a black shadowy figure moving quivering rapidly, he couldn't make out what it was at first. As he neared it, it stopped moving, stopping the priest in his tracks.

'Who are you?' he called to it. The black figure rose, just standing there motionless. 'Who are you?' the priest called again to it. 'What do you want from this house?' The figure then sped past the priest, knocking him to the floor. Picking himself his cross and bible up from the floor he sped out of the bedroom leaving the other rooms fleeing downstairs into the kitchen, picking up his bag and running out through the front door holding his stole, talking into it with one hand and fumbling around in his bag for his car keys with the other hand.

'Everything alright, Pat?' I shouted. 'Did you find anything?'

'Ah no, no, no. I'll call Ann later!' he shouted as he slammed the car door behind him.

'OK,' I said, 'I'll let her—' Before I could finish my sentence he drove off at what you could call a pretty fast pace.

Ann arrived home from shopping and I told her that her boss had gone, he had only been here for about 10 minutes,

'My boss,' she answered.

'Yeah, Father Patrick,' I replied.

'Oh, don't be stupid,' she said. 'You say some really silly things sometimes. I'll call him,' she placed her shopping on the kitchen worktop, picking up the telephone. 'Oh, the phone's dead.' she looked at me,

'I'll report it,' I said.

'mind you I can't even use my mobile as we don't have a bloody signal here do we' said Ann , 'oh I'll call in to the vicarage Thursday' she said.

'I Thought you said the phones not working picking up the phone', And hearing the dial tone 'it's working now I remarked',

'Oh I'll still pop in and see him I prefer to see him face to face anyway 'said Ann disappearing up the stairs to the bedroom,

It was a few days later, I took Ann over to The Oak for a couple of beers, leaving Anthony to look after Leanne.

'Oh, I know what I wanted to tell you,' said Ann. 'I dropped into Mum's yesterday then went on to the vicarage to see Father Patrick. I knocked on the door and Mrs Jones the house keeper answered it. I asked if Father Patrick was in', 'no,' she said, 'he has gone.' 'Gone where,' I said. 'We don't know. He came back from a meeting and packed his bags and left without saying anything', replied Mrs Jones. *Strange*, I thought. I said 'OK, thanks,' got in the car and drove off.'

'What day was that?' I asked.

'That Monday he came round to us,' answered Ann.

'You don't think it had anything to do with us?' I said.

Ann shrugged her shoulders and we carried on drinking.

'Evening, play mates,' came a voice out of nowhere. It was Darren; a nice guy who knew everything and everybody in the village. I told him about our situation. 'I know someone who can help you.' He replied

'Do you?' I said.

'Yeah, her name is Helen, she's a white witch.'

'A what?' I said.

'A white witch' he replied,

'what's that then?' I said

'A good witch,' he said.

'Sod off, you're winding us up.' I joked back at him

'No,' replied Darren, 'no really. I'll get her to come round and have a chat.'

'Yeah OK, whatever,' I said laughing.

'Don't be sceptical,' said Darren, 'give her a chance. She's supposed to be really good.'

'OK,' said Ann. 'Ask her to come round, please, Darren. Any night, preferably Wednesday.'

Three evenings later, Tuesday, there was a knock at the door, followed by a long ring on the door bell. I opened the door to see some lady standing there. She was dressed in a dress which had tassels and bells on it and looking like a sixties hippie. She was about forty-five, long black hair, slim but with the biggest pair of breasts I have ever seen in my life. They were like bowling balls held in a hammock. *Jesus,* I thought, *you could get lost in there*.

'My name is Helen,' she said, interrupting my thoughts. 'I'm Darren's friend. He said you may need my help.'

Lucky Darren, I thought.

‘Hello,’ said Ann appearing from behind me, ’you must be Helen.

‘Yes,’ she said, ‘I was asking your husband if you needed my help.’

‘Come in,’ Ann said, ushering her into the front room and whispering to me as she passed ‘you can put your eyeballs back into your sockets, now go and make a cup of tea there’s a luv.’

Helen was in the living room when Ann caught up to her.

‘Oh, something happened in this room. I can’t make out what but something dreadful,’ she said.

Umm thought Ann.

She then went into the dining room were Mum had stayed first of all.

‘Yes, it’s in here as well.’

‘What is?’ I asked as I walked back in from the kitchen with two cups of tea.

‘There’s an energy, a force here,’ she replied. She went into the kitchen. ‘no nothing in here’ claimed Helen ,’ can I go upstairs now,

‘Please’ said Ann,

Ascending the stairs, she stopped on the mezzanine floor.

‘There’s something there in the corner by the window.’ Said Helen

‘What?’ I said.

‘I don’t know, it’s pure energy. Oh, it’s gone now,’ she replied.

I looked at Ann and smiled. We continued up the stairs onto the landing. She first went into Anthony’s bedroom.

‘There’s been activity in this room.’ Looking at Ann who stared straight back at me. ‘There’s been a presence in here, one or two entities. Let’s carry on,’ she said, entering Leanne’s room. ‘I can’t feel anything in here,’ she said.

‘It’s this room I would have thought that had something wrong,’ I whispered to Ann. ‘Should we tell her about Leanne’s imaginary friend?’

‘No,’ she replied, ‘leave it for now.’

We entered the bedroom Mum had used when she swapped with Glen.

‘No, nothing in here either,’ said Helen. Then walking into our bedroom. ‘There is something in here, it’s here now’, ‘where’ I said, it’s in there ‘replied Helen, pointing to the middle wardrobe then opening the door starring into it,

‘It’s here, it’s a man, a young man. What is it you want?’ she asked. After a pause Helen said, ‘He’s stuck. He can’t get out of the house. What’s your name?’ she said. ‘Oh,’ then mumbled for about thirty seconds, gesticulating all the time. ‘He’s gone now,’ she said. ‘He didn’t know what to do or were to go, poor luv. He said he was looking for his wife and daughter. He said they had gone without him. I have shown him the way out. The energy is no longer there, it’s gone,’ claimed Helen. ‘You should be OK now.’

As she turned towards us, her face changed and her eyes started to stare past us, looking at the wall behind us, following a trail up to the ceiling very slowly. She stood there looking at a dead space on the ceiling.

‘Are you OK,’ Ann asked.

‘Eh yes, yes, I’m fine,’ she said, smiling. ‘Is that the time?’ looking at her watch she said ‘I must go,’ as she made her way past us and down the stairs hastily, followed by me.

‘How much do we owe you?’ I asked her.

‘Nothing,’ came the reply.

‘You sure?’ I asked.

‘Yes I’m sure, no charge,’ she replied.

I said, ‘Did this man give you his name?’ as she went through the front door.

‘Konrad!’ she yelled back as she closed the gate, got into her car and drove off.

‘Konrad,’ I said, still sceptical.

That night I was woken by Anthony.

‘Dad, you awake?’

‘I am now,’ I said. ‘What is it?’

‘I can hear someone downstairs.’

Jumping out of bed I put my dressing gown on and proceeded downstairs followed by Anthony and Ann. We stopped at the bottom of the stairs and listened.

‘Can you hear that? It does sound like voices but I can’t make out what is being said,’ said Ann.

‘It sounds foreign, Dutch? German? It sounds like a kid talking,’ I said.

We entered the living room only to find the room empty but with that smell again.

‘I don’t know,’ I said, ‘I can’t make it out. Glen’s coming over tomorrow, I’ll run it past him.’

The next day Glen arrived to finish the bathroom.

‘Popping over your mums to pick some bits up with Glen, do you need anything while I’m out?’ I said to Ann.

‘No thanks, I’ll let Mum know you’re on your way.’

‘OK, see ya later,’ I said, closing the door behind me. As we drove to the in-laws, I told Glen what had been happening and asked him what he thought.

‘What does Ann say?’ he asked.

‘She doesn’t say much. I think that woman, the witch, coming over scared her a bit,’ I said.

‘I don’t know, mate,’ said Glen, ‘apart from that incident with your mum, I haven’t seen or heard anything when I have stayed over. What I would suggest is if you feel like that you should sell up and go.’

‘I don’t know,’ I replied. ‘We got the house at a very cheap price. Now I can see why. If I did sell we won’t make any profit and we still need to find a place to live.’

‘Look,’ replied Glen, ‘do you like the place?’

‘Yes,’ I replied, ‘but don’t like what’s going on in it.’

‘Well, as I said, if I was you, I would seriously think about selling up, grabbing Ann and the kids and getting the fuck out of there.’

There was a long pause, I said to him eventually, 'We can't afford to leave. We have everything tied up in that house.'

'Go to my parents or your mum's,' was his reply.

'We can't, I said. 'Mum's only got a 1 bedroom flat and your parents have only got a 2-bedroom bungalow. We wouldn't all fit in,' *and to be honest*, I thought to myself, *I would rather take a chance with the ghost then your parents.*

'Well you asked, Lee, and that's what I think,' said Glen.

We had just arrived at the in-laws when the phone rang. It was Ann.

'You need to come home now!' she screamed.

'What is it?' I said.

'There's water pouring through the ceiling.'

'Shit,' I said. 'We're leaving now.'

We made it back to the house within half hour. It was like a storm, water literally pouring through the ceiling.

'I can't turn the stop cock off!' screamed Ann.

'Why?' I shouted back at her.

'I don't know where the fucking thing is.'

'Oh,' I said, throwing myself under the stairs, turning the tap shut. The water stopped, we just stood and looked at the damage.

'I'm going to cry,' said Ann.

'Let's go and see what has happened,' said Glen, heading for the bathroom. 'Oh, Christ,' said Glen, bending down and looking under the bath. 'You know that joint between the pipe and the flexi pipe to the tap?'

'Yeah,' I said.

'Well, it's come apart.'

'How can that happen? It's a compression joint,' I said.

'Christ knows. You insured?' said Glen.

'Don't be silly,' I replied.

'Oh well, said Glen we will have to sort this out ourselves, mate.'

The carpet was soaked, and we had to throw it away, but I wasn't that bothered as I wanted to put laminate flooring down anyway,

'I thought you said this house was built in the 1800s,' said Glen.

'Well, that's what we were told', I said 'Why?' 'I didn't think they had concrete floors in those days' replied Glen,

we noticed now the lump in the floor, it had got bigger,

we left the room to dry out using a couple de-humidifies glen had from his lock – up.

Glen had a job to go to that week so he left leaving us to fend for our self's, 'see you in a couple of weeks' he shouted out of the window of his van let the place dry out completely , ok mate I shouted back ,

The next morning Anthony came down for breakfast.

'Dad, can you stop Leanne from coming into my room. She did it again last night.'

'When did she come in your room?' I said.

'I told you, last night.'

'What time' I said

'I don't know,' he answered. 'About 2 o'clock.'

Leanne entered the kitchen, sat down at the table and poured herself some cornflakes.

'Morning, Mum, morning, Dad, morning, you,' looking at Anthony.

'Leanne, why do you keep going into Anthony's bedroom?' I asked her.

'I haven't,' she replied.

'Yes you have, you did it again last night,' said Anthony, 'and you keep talking to that whatever it is, that cat.'

'No, I never and I don't talk to anybody!' she yelled back at him.

'That's enough now, stop it,' I said. 'You stay out of Anthony's room, Leanne, and you stop telling tales Anthony , now go and get dressed and get ready for school.'

A couple of nights later it was about 1.00 a.m. when I woke to hear Anthony screaming 'get out of here', jumping out of bed and turning the light on. I went into Anthony's room to find him sitting up.

'What's the matter?' I asked him

'She was in my room again, Dad.'

I went into Leanne's room only to find her fast asleep.

'OK,' I said to Anthony, 'go back to sleep, I'll talk to her again in the morning.'

I turned the light off and went back to bed but left the landing table lamp on and my door open.

'What do you think?' Ann said.

'I'm thinking what Helen had said.'

'What, about that thing in his room?' asked Ann

'Yes,' I said, 'try and get some sleep.'

It was about half an hour later, Ann had gone back to sleep and I was laying on my side in bed looking out of the door not thinking about anything in particular, when I noticed from the light of the table lamp something at the end of the passage moving. I couldn't see at first what it was but it was coming closer. It moved very slowly, a dark shadow with no particular shape. It got to about 4 metres from me, I could just make out it was a figure. A little girl. I thought it was Leanne. It came closer and closer; 3 metres, 2 metres. I turned on my table lamp but there was nothing there. I turned the lamp off to see the young girl standing in front of me, her face twisted beyond recognition. I screamed, waking Ann. The girl disappeared.

'What's the matter?' screamed Ann.

I said, 'Nothing, nothing, I just had a bad dream. Go back to sleep, luv.'

We slept with the landing light on from that night onwards.

The next day I started work on the front room, removing the dehumidifiers and lifting the tiles in the bathroom.

'Lee, the phone it's Glen!' shouted Ann.

‘OK, hi, Glen, I have made a start. Tomorrow, OK, see you then, mate. Glen’s coming over tomorrow!’ I shouted to Ann.

‘Yes, I know, he said.’

It had been raining continuously for two days and that evening witnessed a thunderstorm of immense proportions. The lightning was to say a bit intimidating.

‘Are all the windows shut?’ I said to Ann.

‘Of course they are,’ she replied.

It was about 9 o’clock, the kids were in bed.

‘I’ll go and check the kids,’ I said. ‘Then I am going to have an early night.’

‘OK, I’ll switch everything off and see you up there,’ said Ann.

As I entered Leanne’s room, I froze. There was a black figure standing over her looking at her, trying to touch her hair or face with its outstretched arm. As it turned its head towards me its face distorted. I realised it was the figure of the young girl I had seen before.

‘Is she OK?’ whispered Ann as she entered the room behind me.

‘Eh yeah, she’s asleep,’ I answered, turning around to look at Ann, then turning back to see the figure had gone.

‘You alright?’ asked Ann. ‘Looks like you’ve seen a ghost.’

If only you knew, I thought. ‘I’ll check Anthony.’ I said,

‘ok, see you in bed,’ wispered Ann.

That night at about midnight a clap of thunder woke me up. In the flashes of lightning, silhouetted against the bedroom window, there standing at the end of my bed two figures – the little girl and a woman motionless just looking at me, staring at me through their eyeless sockets .As I laid there I could feel the blood draining out of my body. I could see them from lightning and the light from the landing; both their faces were twisted. They stayed for a minute but it seemed like an eternity, and that smell. I didn’t wake Ann.

Glen arrived about 10 a.m. the next morning. I must admit I was glad to see him.

'That was some storm last night,' he stated. , There's a good few roads flooded didn't think I was going to get here, smiling at him and thinking I'm so glad you have,

We started work again and within three days we were laying the floor tiles in the bathroom,

A great job done, now the front room,

Next day we surveyed the living room,

'Lee about this lump in the concrete shall we try and flatten it out' asked glen,

'yeah why not,' just take the top off 'I replied 'and then we can re-float it ',

'I noticed an hair line crack along the top of it so it should go quite easy ' I said, handing glen a brick bolster and hammer I said to him 'be my guest', with that glen gave a sharp hard blow and the concrete fell apart leaving a hole about 30 centimetres round and 22 centimetres deep ,

'Fuck me, Glen,' I said, 'just take the top off, not destroy the bloody foundations.'

Clearing the debris out of the hole we could see the dirt under the house.

'Oh, boy, not sure how we are going to fill this bugger in,' said Glen. 'Wait a minute,' he said, 'what's that? 'what' I said , it looks like an end of a tin , Scrapping away the dirt 'yeah it's an old OXO tin' claimed Glen,

Glen pulled the tin out the hole and handed it to me ,'what's in it' asked glen, 'I don't know the lids stuck' I replied,' try using a flat head screw driver to prise it off' said Glen, 'no it won't move' I said trying to prise the lid off,

'Let me try' Said Glen

Using the hammer, Glen gently tapped the sides of the tin, then using the screwdriver again manged to get the lid off, only for the lid to end up the other end of the room.

'What's in there?' I said. 'some papers which have got some writing on that has faded away' said Glen , a couple of old photos and a couple of coins, foreign, I think, wow look at these producing two crosses and chains They are beautiful,' exclaimed Glen 'they look like gold', He said , one of the crosses was approx. 10.00 centimetres in height and was approx. 5.00 centimetres in width across the cross, the other cross was a bit smaller, they were quite heavy, the top half of the crosses were the same shape as the iron cross worn by the officers in the German army encrusted with diamonds in the shape of a star, the bottom half of the cross was shaped like the base of a Celtic cross solid with an inscription "unsere liebe immer". The chains seemed solid gold.

'We are rich,' said Glen as my eyes turned to the photographs. One of the photos was of a house, or more like a prefab, like those built after WWII to house the homeless in London with 'k 97'? written on the back of it. It looked run down and in decay. The second photograph depicted a woman, on the back was written 'liebe Konrad'. Konrad wait I thought wasn't that the name that Helen the witch had said? Turning the photo back I looked at the woman again. She was very attractive about 20–25, long dark hair, very thin, wearing an awful hat. I stared hard at the photo and my skin ran cold as I thought is this a coincidence or could this be one of the figures I have seen in my nightmares? What could have happened to her?

'Did you hear me?' said Glen. 'We are rich.'

'Yeah,' I said, 'I'm going to look into this', 'what's there to look into its treasure trove' said Glen ,'no I said ,'there's something wrong here very wrong',

Taking the crosses off Glen, I replaced them into the box and stored the box on top of the sideboard.

'Come on, let's fill this hole in,' I said.

Ann arrived home from her parents' a few hours later.

'Ann, here, look at what we have found under the house.'

'Oh, an OXO box, very nice.'

'No, look what's inside.' Looking at the crosses. 'They are beautiful,' she said picking them up out of the tin. 'Whose are they?'

'I believe they belong to her,' I said, showing her the photograph of the young lady.

'Who is she?' asked Ann

'I don't know they must have lived here a long time ago.'

'What are you going to do with them?' she asked.

'Sell them,' shouted Glen, kneeling on the floor, screening the cement.

'Not until I make sure they are not stolen first,' I said.

'How are you going to do that?' Ann said inquisitively.

'I have no idea, and where do I start?' I replied

'Have a word with Jack next door,' suggested Ann. 'He's lived here all his life,' as she replaced the crosses and walked off into the kitchen, followed by me.

'Ann, can you remember the name of that ghost Helen was supposed to have exorcised?'

'Konrad,' she replied.

'Are you sure?' I asked

'Positive,' she said, as I placed the back of the photograph with Konrad written across the back, in front of her face.

'No,' she said, 'that's not possible. God, how did she know that?'

We stood there looking at each other.

The next day I knocked on Jack's front door.

'Who is it?' came a reply.

'It's me Jack, Lee next door.'

'OK, wait a minute.' Eventually he opened the door. 'What is it?' he asked.

'Can you spare a minute, Jack?'

'Yeah, come in,' he answered.

We went into his front room.

'Cup of tea' asked Jack. 'only if you are making one mate,' I said.

As he shuffled to his kitchen I sat looking around the room. It was quite a big room; a big fireplace with a beautiful clock that sat on the mantelpiece over the fire.

'It's German,' said Jack. 'Kettle's just boiling.' As he shuffled back into the living room.

'It's lovely,' I said.

'Yes, it was given to my father many years ago. 'Anyway, what can I do for you?' asked Jack

'I have got a question', I said ,'do you know anything about my house, Cedar Cottage?'

'Like what?' he asked.

'Well, it's supposed to be 18th century but I don't think it is.' I said

'Why?' said Jack.

'Well, the floor is concrete and I don't think concrete was around that time.'

'Concrete has been around since the Romans, even earlier,' he said, laughing, as he shuffled back into the kitchen to make the tea. 'My parents bought this house back in 1910 or 1911, not long before the great war and as far back as I can remember your house has stood where it is,' he shouted from the kitchen. 'My father said to me that your house had burned down in 1918. Not sure how or what caused it. It had been rented to a German family who came over here and that's all I know,' Jack said as he emerged back into the living room carrying two cups of tea. 'It stood derelict till about 1921 then David Charles the farmer had it knocked down. The plot stayed empty until about 1938 when your house was built. I remember that because I was about ten and I was shouted at by the builder for playing in his sand and with some bricks. I got a swift clip round my ear from Dad for being naughty.' He laughed and sipped his tea. '1939, the Second World War started and it stood empty. I joined the army in 1948 National Service for a year but stayed on for another two years. When I got de-mobbed, I came home, and your house was occupied. Wilson was the name of the family. They didn't stay long – about six months if I can remember rightly. In 1952, Charles sold most of his land to a developer who built the rest of the village. He died in 1958 and was buried in St Mary's.

'Your house was occupied another three times, if I can remember rightly, in the 1960s no one seemed to stay that long. My mum and dad thought it was a council house and these people were using it as a halfway house. In the seventies it was again left empty. A housing association bought it in early 1980s; again, it had its fair share of tenants but something must have happened in 1998 when the housing association sold the house. The house was bought in 2001, or might be 2002, by a family called Williams. It was six months, if that, they sold up and moved. Don't know who bought it; it could have been repossessed by the bank, I don't really know'. Said Jack 'in 2004 it was again sold or let out this time to a young couple who in late 2004 left during the night I think it was 2004 could have been 2005 again I'm not really sure'. Said Jack 'Wow' I said, 'They woke us up about 1 o'clock in the morning, speeding away in their car, it has stayed empty until you moved in'. said Jack

'I don't wish to worry you, Lee,' he said, 'but when we spoke to some of the tenants, all of them claim to have seen something that scared them.'

'Did they say what they had seen?' I asked.

'A young girl and a lady,' replied Jack.

'Hmm,' I said.

'Why? Have you seen anything?' he asked.

'No,' I said, 'nothing at all. Anyway, I'll make some enquires see if I can find anything locally or on the internet. I should go now Ann will be wondering where I have got to , thanks for the tea and the gossip, Jack,' trying to make light of what he had said, thinking 'oh shit' to myself

'Well, take care Lee', said Jack as I was leaving, 'Oh that clock was given to my parents by the German family who lived in your house, their name was Becker, I think. Yes, it was, I'm sure it was. They were supposed to have been a very nice couple. They had a little girl, according to my dad.' Said Jack.

'Thanks again Jack'. I said and left.

'Well?' said Ann, as I arrived home. 'Did he know anything?'

'He said that a German family called Becker lived here in the early 1900s, and various families have lived here since then. He was a bit vague about the dates though'. i said , ' I have a feeling that the Beckers had money – you want to see the clock they gave him and those crosses must have cost them something. I'll look on the internet to see if I can get any inspiration.'

'Try National Archives or Land Registry,' said Ann, 'or that company that advertise on the telly.'

'Ummm yeah I know the one,' I said.

That evening, 'are you coming to bed?' said Ann as I sat at my computer.

'Yeah, I replied in a minute, just finishing up.'

'What are you doing?' she asked.

'Just trying to look for something about this place.'

'Well, don't stay up too late, you have work tomorrow.'

'Yeah, like I didn't know,' I said. I spent approximately four hours a night for the next three nights researching the history of Cedar Cottage and surrounding area. On Saturday night I thought *sod it, I'll watch the football.*

'What are you doing?' said Ann.

'I'm going to put my feet up and watch the football,' I said.

'Oh, I'm going to bed then. I'll watch the telly in bed.' Said Ann

'OK, brilliant, I thought, *no nagging*. So, with a can of lager and a packet of cheese and onion crisps I sat down to watch the games. It was about half an hour, maybe three quarters of an hour, into the programme I noticed something out of the corner of my eye. Turning my head towards it, a shadowy figure was rising from the corner of the room, against the wall by the window. It stood up erect, standing at about 2 meters and motionless.

Transfixed, I continued to look at it. Suddenly it came towards me, gliding across the floor very, very slowly. As it got nearer it sped up to me very quickly. I was pinned to the chair; I couldn't move; I couldn't breathe. I was terrified.

It stopped in front of me, placing its hands on my shoulders and pressing me into the chair then leaning towards me its shoulders arching and its head dropping, its face edging, getting closer to my face. I tried to scream but nothing came out. It stopped inches away from face. As i stared into its face I realised It was not twisted as before, it was burnt, really burnt. I couldn't distinguish if it was male or female. As I looked into its empty eye sockets I could feel terror, sorrow, pain, helplessness. I remember just feeling numb. It moved its face away from mine and lifted its hands away from my shoulders. It was then I regained my voice and I screamed. It left as quick as it arrived.

'What is it?' screamed Ann, running down the stairs followed closely by Anthony and Leanne.

'What's the matter, Daddy'? said Leanne.

'You alright, Dad?' said Anthony.

'Yeah, I'm fine, kids. I fell asleep, just had a bad dream that's all. Thanks. Go back to bed now.' I said.

As they ascended the stairs Ann said 'What's wrong? What happened? This is the second time you have had this nightmare.'

'They weren't nightmares, they were real,' I said. It was then that a sense of sadness descended on me and I started to cry, sobbing into her shoulder. I said to Ann, 'Those poor people were in the house when it caught fire, they died here. Oh my god, they were burnt alive.' Ann put her arms around me and we just sat there.

A few days later, Wednesday I think, Glen came round in the evening, grabbing a cup of tea that Ann had made him and then sitting down on the sofa next to her.

'So, what have you found out about the house?' he asked.

Turning away from the computer I replied, 'Well, according to the Land Registry, the house, along with Jack's next door and all the subsequent houses, about twenty-four in all, was owned by David Charles the farmer. He owned all the land around here as well, quite a character, he was also the local magistrate.'

'Oh, an arsehole then,' claimed Glen.

'If I can finish,' I interrupted. 'By all accounts he was well liked and a very generous man. He was a businessman; owned and rented out some of the shops in Rochford. He built the memorial hall for the village and supported St Mary's church, where he is buried. He sold the land off in the 1950s and they built the rest of the village, along with the pub. By all accounts this village was classed as a hamlet before then. It had just a dirt track as the road. This road – the B9696 – was built about the same time as the new houses in the 1950s. I said. According to the UK census in April 1911 the family who lived here was known as Becker, as Jack had said. There was the father, Konrad.'

'the name on the back of that photo!' exclaimed Glen.

'Right,' I replied. 'His wife's name was Anna.'

'A bit of a coincidence,' said Ann 'they had a daughter Katarina born 1904 or 1905' I said ,' leanness invisible friend cat' said Glen , 'it's not a cat that Anthony thought it's that little girl Katarina' Ann said , 'yeah' I said 'you are probably right,' 'Spooky' said Glen, 'obviously Anna is the lady in the photo' I said, 'according to jack the house burnt down in 1918 and I think the family perished in it Katarina would have been about 13 maybe 14 bless her I said, so sad said Ann ,

'How did the fire start?' said Glen.

'Jack had no idea,' I said.

'Can't you ask him when the house was re-built?' said Glen.

'He told me the other day it was about 1938, I think. I'm not sure. I'll speak to him again later,' I replied.

‘Don’t leave it too long, he’s getting on a bit. He might not be around much longer,’ said Glen, laughing.

A few days later the bell rang and I answered the door, it was Jack.

‘Hi, Jack, what’s up?’ I asked.

‘There’s something I want to tell you, which I should have done the other day.’ He said.

‘Yeah, OK,’ I said, sounding inquisitive. ‘Come in, sit down. Want a cup of tea?’

‘Yes please,’ he replied. I went to make some tea then sat down opposite him,

‘My father died in 1946, just after the Second World War. I was seventeen. It was just before I had to do National Service; can’t remember exactly, the brain cells, you know. He died of TB, well, complications due to TB.’

‘Sorry to hear that, Jack,’ I said.

‘He was laid up in bed for some time before he died and I would go and sit with him for a few hours a day, and we would just talk about nothing particular’, said Jack. Then one evening just before he died he said he wanted to tell me about something that happened that he was ashamed of and had been regretting for the past fifty years’, something he should have done or prevented from happening but didn’t. “What was it, Dad?” I asked. “Well, it was 1914, Konrad and Anna, as you know, lived in this house before the fire they had a baby girl. Katarina they called her,” my dad said. “She was lovely.’ said Jack

‘You didn’t tell me you knew their first names, only Becker,’ I said to Jack.

‘Yes, well,’ Jack said sheepishly , he continued ‘Dad was putting the rubbish out one morning when he bumped into Konrad as he was going to work – he was a baker and worked at Brights the bakers in Rochford. After exchanging “mornings” Konrad said “have you heard about the assassination of Ferdinand?”, Archduke Franz Ferdinand and his wife Sophie were shot and killed in Sarajevo, Austria/Hungry declared war against Serbia and Germany, the rest is history said Jack.

Thanks for the history lesson, I thought, *get on with it.*

"'I think there will be trouble over there," said Konrad. Dad told him that he had heard. "Just as well you are here," he said. "Yes, I am so grateful to be here with my family." With that, Konrad went on his way. 'On the 4th of august 1914 Germany invaded Belgium the war for Britain the great war, ww1 had begun,' said Jack. 'Although there was an amazing turnout of volunteers by those brave, brave men, things wasn't going so well and we lost thousands of soldiers. In 1916 conscription was introduced through the Military Service Act and any able lad between seventeen and forty-one had to fight. You know you could have refused to fight,' said Jack, 'but that was looked down on and you had to attend these tribunals to prove that you had a genuine case of conscience, whether religious or political.'

'Right,' I said.

'Thousands of men were deemed conscientious objectors and were assigned to the non-combatant corps. Dad called it such as medics or civilian labour,' said Jack.

'Really? That's interesting,' I said, trying to move the story along at a quicker pace.

'A letter was sent to all the tenents of Stambridge, except for the Beckers, due to them being German,' he said. 'They were lucky, as the government deported most of the Germans throughout the war, you know. In 1917, even the Royal Family changed their name from Saxe-Coburg to Windsor.'

'Really?' I said.

'Yes,' he replied.

Ann smiled and handed him another cup of tea.

Jack continued 'dad said all the tenants had to attend the meeting called by David Charles at the memorial hall'. *All are to attend at 17.30 by order of His Majesty George V*, demanded the letter,

'Everyone attended. On a stage that had been built was a long table; at the head was David Charles. Behind the table, looking at the residents, were an army officer named

Davies and a weasel-looking character named Kite from the Home Office and the Reverend John Owens, vicar of St Mary's. "Ladies and gentlemen, quite please," said David Charles as he stood up from the table. "You have been summoned here for a reason. I will hand you over to Captain Davies. Captain?"

"Thank you, sir' said Captain Davies,' Ladies, gentlemen, as you know the war in France is still active and as you are aware, we have initiated a plan for conscription. I have letters for men of fighting age to attend Aldershot Barracks for immediate training to fight for their country. I will hand you over to Mr Kite. Mr Kite?"

"Thank you, Captain." Said Kite

Jack continued 'dad said four lads had been identified and were to leave the next morning. They were twins Robert and Alfred Smith, 17, Alfred Jones, 18, Steven Harrison, 17'.

'"No!" screamed Martha Smith as she sobbed into her handkerchief in one hand and clutched at her boys with the other.

''Why?" said James Smith, the twins' father. "Why do you have to take our sons?"

'"Because their country needs them," replied Captain Davies.

'"Why should we fight for the bloody French? What have they ever done for us?" shouted Sidney Harrison, Steven's father.

'"Please, ladies and gentlemen, could we have some calm," said the reverend Owens.

'We made a promise to the Belgium people continued captain Davies that we would stand with them if in event of an invasion by Germany and that is what has happened,"

'"Subsequently, we have recognised five more lads who will be coming to the age of seventeen next year, They will be enlisted into the armed forces," said Kite.

“and will receive their call-up papers through the post. Thank you, goodnight.”

Dad said ‘With that they all left the stage, leaving the parents to quarrel and bicker amongst themselves.

‘“If anyone would like communion you are welcome at St Mary’s,” said the vicar.

‘My dad said there was a service at St Mary’s next morning to wish the boys good fortune, then they gave the lads a bloody good send-off. All the residents were there, including the Beckers.

‘“What do you want here?” said Reg Smith, the twins’ uncle.

‘“Yeah, piss off back to Germany, you bastards!” shouted Sidney Harrison.

‘My dad shouted leave them alone. “This bloody war is not their fault.”

‘“You can piss off as well,” said Harrison.

‘With that Mum and Dad and the Beckers left and walked home.

The Beckers didn’t leave the house much after that, only for Konrad to go to work. My parents were probably the only friends they had’.

‘It was a few weeks later’ Jack continued, my mother Elizabeth met Martha Smith, the twins’ mother, while shopping in Rochford.

‘“How are the boys?” said Mum.

‘“Well, thank you’,she replied ‘ they have joined the 12th (Eastern) division and have been sent to some place called the Western Front. I think that’s what Alfred called it a couple of days ago. It’s in France, a town called Arras. The boys are all together though.”

‘“Oh, that’s good,” said Mum, “give them my love when you write to them.”

‘“I will,” said Martha as they carried on their way.

‘It was sometime in November 1917 we got the message Robert and Alfred Jones had been killed in action at Monchy-le-Preux in Arras. By January 1918 all four boys were dead. Alfred and Steven killed in action at

Wancourt-Feuchy, Arras. A sense of gloom and despondency fell on Stambridge as we all came to terms we would never see those boys again. They were good lads, respected by everyone, loved by their parents, now gone, and not forgetting the lads that were going to be seventeen in a few months in 1918. They say time is a healer but someone forgot to tell the people of Stambridge,' said Jack.

'As time went on, sorrow and despondence was replaced by anger and revenge and the only target at hand was the Becker family. It started at first with verbal abuse followed by the graffiti on the walls and doors, then smashing of windows. Eventually, the Beckers became prisoners in their own house. Mum and Dad were there for them, although Dad said he was spat at and called a few names by some of the residents but it didn't deter him. That's when the Beckers gave him the clock, you know,' sipping his tea, 'as a thank you, Dad rejected it at first but they begged him so he accepted it.,' Jack said.

'It was February or March, I can't remember the exact month for sure 'said Jack,' Dad said to me when it happened.' There was a long pause.

'What?' I asked. 'What happened?'

'It was about 7 o'clock in the evening when a crowd of people turned up outside the Becker house' my dad said.

'Jones and Harrison were there, he saw them. They were shouting and jeering. He looked out the window and watched them. Said Jack

Dad stood there for at least ten minutes watching them hurl abuse and stones at the house.

'"You should go out there and tell them to stop," Mum said.

'"And do what?" dad said.

"Hopefully they will go home in minute' he said. To be honest with you, Jack, I was scared," he said.

'Dad said he left the house and ran across the field to get David Charles who dispatched a farm hand to run to Rochford to get the police.

Charles and Dad headed back to the Beckers' across the field. When they got there the Beckers' house was on fire and the mob had gone,' said Jack.

'My mum ran out of our house to meet Dad and Charles screaming and crying. "Help them, they are still in there," she begged, pointing to the Beckers' house. 'We tried to enter the house', Said Dad,' but were beaten back by the heat and the flames. We could hear screaming from inside the house, it was terrible, we couldn't get to them. We just stood there shocked, feeling helpless. I just stood there cuddling your mum who was sobbing profusely 'said Dad.

'The police arrived eventually along with the fire brigade but by the time they arrived the house was gutted, the fire was almost out'.

Jack continued, 'Dad said 'the police were banging on doors of the villagers and started taking statements, obviously a code of silence had spread around the hamlet'.

'Detective Sergeant Davidson – I think that was his name' said Jack 'asked Dad whether he knew any of the mob. Although Dad recognised Jones and Harrison for sure he said no'.

'"I lied," said Dad. "I should have told the truth but I was scared they may come after your mum and me, I should have done more, I should have gone out and stopped them instead of cowering under the window like a coward and running away."

'You went to get help. You have nothing to recriminate yourself with." Said Jack, Dad replied "maybe".

Finishing his tea and placing his cup and saucer on to the side table Jack continued.

'Dad said that they did a thorough investigation but the verdict was inconclusive. There was no smell or sign of arson. We knew the Beckers used candles,' he sighed. 'Maybe it was an accident but reg Harrison threw that brick through their window I saw him do it just before I ran away to get help'. 'Dad you did the right thing'.

Jack continued 'The Beckers were buried at St Mary's together. A small service was held by the vicar John Owens, Mum and Dad were there, along with about two dozen other residents. None of the Harrisons were there; too ashamed, I hope. It was not long after that my dad died. I think he was glad to get it off his chest and tell someone the family may have been murdered.

"Why haven't you told the police yourself?' I asked.

'What's the point?' said Jack', A few of the villagers left the village sometime after that. Reg and Sid are both dead now probably, all the others are as well.'

'Yeah, but you could have got closure.' I said

'Who knows?' said Jack. 'It could have been an accident; .

1938 as I said the other day or near that said Jack,

'What is?' I asked.

'When your house was built.' Said Jack

'How did you know I was going to ask you that?' I said.

'I spoke to Ann the other day,' replied Jack, smiling at her.

I already knew that from the Land Registry site but it was nice of him to tell me again, I thought.

'That was sad,' Ann said as he left.

'Yeah, very,' I replied. 'Fancy a walk to the church in the morning? See if we can find the Beckers' graves tomorrow, luv?'

'Yeah, why not?' said Ann.

The next morning, we walked, well, nearly walked to the church. We felt a spot of rain and took refuge in the car; mind you, it only took a couple of minutes to get there, where as if we walked it would have taken me about half an hour what with my dodgy knees. We went through the arch then the gate into the grounds of St Mary's.

'Jesus, where do you start looking, look at all those headstones.' I said

'Well, you start by not blaspheming,' said Ann.

'If you take that side of the church and I will take this side,' I said.

'OK, what am I looking for?'

'Are you kidding? A headstone,' I said.

'What is written on it, Einstein?' joked Ann.

'I don't know, look for Becker. Can't be many of them in here.

Ann strolled off in her direction and I stated looking at the headstones in front of me. I had looked for about twenty minutes when I came across a headstone; very dirty with moss and weeds growing over it. I bent down on the grave itself and started scraping away the decay.

'Get off,' came a voice from nowhere.

'What?' I said, tumbling over on to my side.

'Get off the grave,' said the voice again.

It can't be, I thought, looking down at the weeds.

'Are you looking for someone?'

I turned around to see a young woman about 30–35, tall, dressed in black with a white collar around her neck.

'Sorry,' I said, 'you startled me. My name is Lee Carpenter. I was just looking for someone who's buried here.'

'Hi, I'm Jessica Fletcher.'

'The mystery writer,' I quipped.

'No, the vicar of St Mary's,' she said with a smile. 'Actually, my mother liked her in *Murder She Wrote* and as our surname is Fletcher, she called me Jessica.'

I laughed. 'This is my wife Ann,' as she came up to be nosy. 'This is Jessica, Jessica Fletcher.'

'Oh, the myst—'

Before she could finish, 'Yes we have done that already,' I said. 'We are looking for a family that died in 1918, they are buried here somewhere.'

'Have you their name?' said Jessica.

'Becker.'

'Let's check the records. If you would follow me, we have a plan of who is buried where in the vestry.' She took us through the front door up to the alter then into a room or should I say an office.

'May I say,' I said, 'that your church is beautiful. I love those stained glass windows.'

'Yes, it is beautiful. It was built in the 15th century and is Grade II listed,' she said as she rummaged through a filing cabinet. '1918,' you said.

'Yes,' I replied .

'Right here is 1900 to 1920, they must have been one of the last burials we had here.' Opening the ledger she said 'Becker. Oh, there was a child as well.'

'Yes, Katarina.'

'That's very sad,' said Jessica. 'Right, they will be plot 207 – 8–9. They should be at the back of the church, top right-hand corner, next to the tree.'

'Thank you,' we said and made our way back to the door.

'There's the tree,' said Ann, looking across the grounds.

We walked to where the graves were.

'It's a bit overgrown. I think that's the headstone there,' said Ann.

'Yes,' I said, bending down to look. 'Yeah, at the top of the headstones, Konrad/Anna and Katarina Becker,' I read out. 1918, was taken by a tragic accident, the headstones also read. Or was it? I thought. 'I tell you what, it's Saturday tomorrow let's come back with some tools and tidy up here.'

'OK,' said Ann.

We spent the whole weekend clearing the plots. The headstones came up really nicely with a bit of elbow grease. Even Jessica commented. 'Don't you have a groundsman?' I said to her.

'We don't have the money,' she replied. 'We rely on people like you to do it voluntarily.'

The issue I had now what to do with those crosses. Glen wanted to sell them, Looking at the photo of Anna, the crosses weren't ours; I wanted to return them to their family where they came from, but how was I going to do that? I thought.

'Where are the crosses?' I asked Ann.

'Glen took them to be valued.'

'He did what?' I said.

'He asked me and I said yes.'

'Why?' I said.

'Why not?' came the reply.

'Because they are not ours. I said

He's not selling them,' said Ann.

The week went by with no incidents.

It was Friday night.

'Are you coming to bed?' said Ann.

'No, I couldn't find anything about the Beckers or this place at the library today, I'm going online to see if I have better luck ',

'OK, see you up there.'

'OK,' I said, putting on some music.

'Keep that down!' shouted Ann from the top of the stairs.

'OK,' I said, turning it down a couple of turns.

A couple of hours past. Thinking *I haven't got a clue here*, I felt a shiver through my back up into my neck. There was something behind me. Turning around, there was the figure of the little girl Katarina. She was just standing there next to the sideboard where I kept the OXO tin. The strange thing was, I wasn't scared. I sat there looking, feeling remorse for this little girl that had died so tragically in that fire.

'Help me please,' I said to her.

The tin fell off the sideboard then she left. I picked up the tin and thought *is there something in here that I have not seen that can help me?* Glen still had the crosses. *I need them back*, I thought, looking at the photos. 'There's got to be something here that I have missed. I said to myself, now where's that bloody magnifying glass'? Looking though the desk. cupboard, drawers, finally finding it in Ann's sewing box. 'Right, let's look' I said.

Holding the photo of Anna In my left hand, and magnifying glass in my right hand I began to study the photo. I couldn't see anything obvious at first, then I noticed in the background, which was grey in colour, in the top left-hand corner, was *o s s e?* and the top right hand a part semi-circle, like the porthole of a ship. *Could it be a ship?* I thought. I entered on my keyboard ships from Germany 1900. Nothing. Re-entering passenger ships from Germany 1885 , Still nothing. '1890'. Nothing. Checking the back of the other photo. The building, could it have been taken at a dock? Wait a minute, *K 97,* I thought to myself. Let's try 1897. To my amazement *SS Kaiser Wilhelm der Grosse, appeared.*

The last four letters o s s e, to much of a coincidence I thought 'I think this is the ship,' I mumbled to myself.

Entering into the keyboard 'Kaiser Wilhelm der Grosse', it brought up a web page Kaiser Wilhelm der Grosse 1897–1914. It told me all about the ship, when it was built and was owned by NDL north-German-Lloyd or Norddeutscher Lloyds, then sold on to the steamship company in late 1897, the web page continued -The ship was constructed at Bremerhaven Germany, or Prussia as it was known then. Its maiden voyage was from Bremerhaven to New York via *Southampton.*

Looking up Kaiser Wilhelm der Grosse passenger list 1897 on the steamship archive web page, there they were the names Konrad and Anna Becker. 'That's them.' I thought.

A few days later, Glen came in through the back door.

'It's only me.'

'Where are those crosses and coins?' I asked.

'Give me a chance to get in,' he said, taking a lager out of the fridge and swigging down a mouthful. 'Sit down, I have found out some facts about those coins,' he said.

Ann entered the room.

'Sit down,' said Glen to her. 'These coins, they are 20 mark gold coins dated 1895.'

'Well, we know that,' I said.

‘Yeah, from Hamburg’ said Glen, ‘so that family almost certainly came from Hamburg.’

‘How do you know that?’ I said.

‘Because, according to the man behind the counter at the jewellers he said the likes of Hamburg, Bremen, he did say some others I can’t remember, they were free cities and had their own coat of arms on their coins’. ‘Worth anything ‘asked Ann,’ a couple of hundred quid’ said Glen. ‘As for the crosses’ he said, they were probably bespoke, as the jeweller had never seen anything like them before. The inscription on them unsere liebe immer stands for “our love always”.’

‘How did you know that?’ said Ann.

‘ Google translate, sis that new site on the internet’ said Glen . They are worth a couple of grand.’

‘Well done. Thanks, Glen,’ I now know how and when they arrived here in this house and were from, I said

‘Well, tell us,’ said Ann, expectantly.

I said. ‘The family must have left Hamburg, arriving at bremer; then from bremer to Bremerhaven. I would imagine by train. They boarded the Kaiser Wilhelm II der Grosse and sailed on its maiden voyage on the 19th of September 1897 and arrived at Southampton on the 20th September 1897. Konrad was nineteen and Ann was twenty-one, according to the ship’s records. I also know they were in our house on the 11th April 1911 because of the UK 1911 census. Their names were on it. They must have had Katarina about 1904, as Jack said. Konrad would have been twenty-four. Ann would have been twenty-six when they moved in here, where they were between 20th September and 11th April before that I don’t know.’

‘Wow, this is really taking you over,’ said Ann.

‘Yeah,’ I said. ‘All I need to know is why they came here.’

A week went by and I had no luck on the internet. To be honest, I only spent a couple of days investigating; the rest of the time working. By the time I got home, I was too tired to research and had some early nights.

Glen phoned me one evening.

'Hi, mate, I'm doing a conservatory for a family in Foxhall, Ipswich and you never guess what?'

'What?' I said.

'They are German, well the husband is.'

'Oh yeah,' I said.

'I was talking to this guy about your predicament and he told me to tell you try going online to this site. You got a pen as I will have to spell it out as I haven't got a clue how you pronounce it.' Said Glen

'OK, fire away,' I said.

'Right, it is o r t s f a m i l i e n b u c h e r.

'Ortsfamilienbucher.' I said,

'Yes,' said Glen. 'I'm sure that's what he called it. You enter that and follow the instructions. The problem is it may all be in German.'

'I'll run it through google translate,' I said. 'May take time but I'm in no hurry. Thanks, Glen, you're a star.'

'Good luck,' he said and put the phone down.

'Who was that?' Ann said.

'Your brother.' I replied

'Oh, what did he want?'

'He gave me a website to go on. I'll do it tomorrow.' I said,

The next day I was on my rota day off so that morning at about 11 o'clock I went online. I entered 'ortsfamilienbucher' and a web page came up in German. 'Gesamtliste der familiennamen' using my translator meant, list the surnames?. I typed in Becker, and pressed enter, geburtsorte auswaertiger personen, birth places external action people?, came the reply entering, Hamburg, harburg/elbe ?,please re-enter surname came the reply ,entering Becker again a list of beckers appeared. I knew he was nineteen because of the ship's records so I entered Konrad Becker 1868. To my surprise, his name came up on screen. Born 14th April 1868 Hamburg; mother and father Karl and Helga Becker. *Could this be him?* I thought. Let's try marriages. I re-entered all the details this time marriages ,but what date should I enter, thinking they were very young could have been running away in which case you wouldn't want to be waiting , I entered 1896 nothing , I then entered 1897 ,They were there. Konrad Becker and Anna Schmaker, married August 24th 1897 at St Michelle's Hanseantic Protestant Church, Hamburg, only four weeks before sailing to England. The church records read Konrad Becker age 19 backer translated (baker) , parents karl becker 42 arbeitslos (unemployed), Helga becker 41hausfrau(housewife), Married , Anna shumaker age 21 jungfer (spinster) , parents horst schumaker Schuster (shoemaker) frieda schumaker Schuster (shoemaker). I had found them. Could it be this easy? I asked myself.

'How are you doing?' asked Ann.

'Really well,' I answered. 'I'm going to concentrate on Anna; it seems her family were cobblers.'

'What?' said Ann.

'COBBLERS,' I said. 'Shoemakers.'

''That's what I thought you said. So how are you going to research her sitting down next to me', said Ann, 'I'll go on-line and see what comes up in Hamburg tomorrow.' I said

The next evening, entering 'shoemakers in Hamburg Germany' into my browser it displayed a list of shoemakers and repairers. In amongst the names was schumaker shoe and boot company established 1830. Reading the history, Horst schumaker founded the shoe boot and leather company with his wife frieda schumaker that's them I thought.

'I think i have found them and they are still trading,' I said to Ann.

'Write to them,' she said

'I feel silly. What am I going to write?'

'What has happened,' said Ann.

'do they have an address' she said, yes its 48 borwerkstraden Karolinenviertel hamburg , they even have an e,mail address I replied ,

Then write to them Ann said again,

'I'll write to them tomorrow,' I said.

The next evening, I sat at my computer thinking how am I going to explain what I need to know? Shall I be clever and write some German or would that be too patronising. No, better not, I thought.

'Here goes nothing,' I mumbled under my breath.

I began, Good evening, my name is Lee Carpenter, I pounded on my keyboard. *I know this may be a strange request, I am enquiring if you know of an Anna Schumaker, born approximately 1865. She came to England in 1897 when she was twenty-one, with her husband Konrad Becker, as I am trying to locate her relatives, thank you.*

It was a couple of days later that I got a reply. It read:

Thank you for your email, Mr Carpenter. My name is Miriam Grubber. I am aware of an Anna Schumaker. Could you please telephone me on this number: 00-49-040-7269977 to discuss this, thank you.

I replied. 'When would be the best time to call you?'

Almost immediately she wrote 'Now would be a good time for me.'

Oh shit, I thought, *what am I going to say?*

'Ann, this lady, Miriam Grubber, wants me to phone her.'

'When?' answered Ann

'Now,' I said.

'Well, phone her then for god's sake' said Ann

'What am I going to ask her?'

'Just talk to her,' said Ann, dialling the number off my computer screen.

The phone was answered almost immediately.

'Good evening,' I said, could I speak to Mrs Grubber?'

'Is that Mr Carpenter?' a voice answered. She spoke very softly and slowly with that hard German accent you expect to hear.

'Yes, I said.'

'You may call me Miriam if you care to.'

'Please call me Lee.'

'Thank you,' she said, 'you will have to excuse my English, Lee.'

'Not at all, your English is better than my German,' I replied. She laughed, which seemed to break the ice so to speak. I felt more relaxed.

She said, 'Our family had an Anna Schumaker a very long time ago. She was my great-great cousin. My grandmother was her mother's sister. My grandmother's name was Ingrid and Anna's mother was Frieda.'

'Yes, I knew her name was Freida from the marriage certificate records from St Michelle's.' I said,

'Then you know Anna and Konrad were married.' Said Miriam

'Yes,' I replied.

'In 1904 or thereabouts they had a baby, a little girl.' I said

'Yes,' said Miriam. 'Katarina.'

'I think I should let you know now, I have some tragic news to tell you concerning the family.' I said,

'What?' said Miriam in anticipation.

'I am afraid to say they died in a terrible accident.'

'How?' said Miriam.

'In 1918, the house they were living in caught fire and they couldn't get out. As I said, I believe it to be a terrible accident.' I didn't want to say possible arson as she didn't need to know that at this present time.

'Oh, that is so, so sad,' said Miriam.

There was a short pause that seemed to last about an hour.

'Are you OK?' I asked her.

'Yes. We often wondered what had happened to them,' came the reply.

'Could you answer a very important question for me please?' I said.

'What is that?' said Miriam.

'Why they left Germany and all their family and friends.'

‘It’s a long and sad story,’ explained Miriam.

‘May I ask why?’ I asked.

‘Why?’ she said.

‘I have worked very hard to trace the family and have spent hours researching them. I know it sounds strange but I feel I know them. I would like to know why they left.’

There was even greater pause then she said, ‘My mother told me as it was told to her by my grandmother. It started three years before they married and left for England. Konrad was a baker in town. He was very young and good looking. Anna was in town with friends. They stopped at the bakery to buy some bread when Konrad and Anna saw each other. They say it was love at first sight. They started seeing each other until her father—’

‘Horst,’ I interrupted.

‘Yes,’ she said. ‘He was told by one of his office clerks whose son knew Konrad. Konrad had boasted to the clerks son about his new girlfriend, a girl called Anna Schumaker. Horst flew into a rage; he wasn’t a nice man. He was forty-nine, very tall, not very big how you say muskel, um, muscle. He followed her one night as she slipped out of the house and he caught them together near Konrad’s home. He nearly killed Konrad. He ordered Anna never to see him again. Anna defied him and carried on seeing Konrad. He disowned her and never spoke to her again. He would not even attend their wedding. Frieda begged him to change his mind but he never did. Konrad and Anna married at St Michelle’s. Both my grandmother and Frieda attended, along with Konrad’s parents Karl and Helga. Horst never attended. he missed his daughter’s wedding and he never saw her again. So sad,’ said Miriam.

‘Yes,’ I agreed.

‘It broke Frieda’s heart, although my grandmother never said, the reason for horst’s anger , we don’t think it was about religion. Anna was a Catholic and Konrad was a Protestant. It may be probably that she was the heiress to the company and would own it eventually and he, Horst, wanted her to marry someone in their how you say, um, klasse.'

'Class,' I said.

'Yes, stature, circle, I don't know. Konrad was not in that class/stature. They stayed at Konrad's home until they left for England,' said Miriam. 'In 1908 or 1909 Frieda received a letter from Anna after Katarina was born. She sent a photograph of Katarina, she was about four. She was so beautiful. Anna said that they were happy; Konrad had got a job at a bakers in Rochford and she (Anna) had made friends and Katarina had become very naughty. The letter went on for three pages. Frieda was so happy she showed the letter to my grandmother. There were a few letters to and from Germany, then in 1914 there were none obviously due to the war. They never heard from them again. They often wondered what had happened. Anna did say they were thinking of returning to Germany when the time was right. Frieda never showed Horst any of the letters. Frieda died in 1933, followed by Horst in 1934. That's all I can tell you,' said Miriam.

'Thank you,' I said. 'I am sorry to have been the bearer of bad news. Would you have a picture of Konrad and Anne I could have please', I asked, 'you can have a copy of the wedding photograph and a copy of the photograph of little katarina also', 'thank you' I said 'no thank you', said Miriam auf wiedersehen ,

I put down the hand set. We had spent about two hours talking on the phone. Christ, I hate to think what my phone bill will be, I said to myself.

'Everything OK?' said Ann. 'You were on there a long time.'

'Yeah,' I said, then I told Ann all that Miriam had said in a condensed form.

'That's sad, 'Don't you ever do that to our kids.' said Ann

'I have no intention,' I replied.

Speaking to Glen a week later, we decided to send the box, including the photos and papers that were very faded, and of course the cross and chains to Miriam. Emailing her, I asked for her address because 'I had something that I felt she should have'.

'210 Walderseesra ottensen altona Hamburg, postcode 22767,' she replied.

I posted the parcel at our local Parcel Force depot in Chelmsford and four days later I received an email from Miriam.

'*Thank you so much* ', said Miriam *'my mother had spoken to me about some Crosse's and chains, these must be them, the crosses and chains were a gift to each other on their wedding day, how did you find them she asked.*

I wrote back*: They were buried under my house. We found them when we were repairing the floor. It's hard to believe they were there for a hundred years.*

Yes, she replied. *Yes, thank you again*, she wrote.

We ended the emails.

'What did she say?' asked Ann.

'She was pleased,' I said.

It was a few weeks later I got a phone call from Miriam.

'Hi, Lee, I've been thinking about Anna, Konrad and little Katarina, and I would like to see their graves so I have decided that I am coming to England, I would be grateful if you would be so kind as to show me their graves.'

'OK, of course I will,' I replied. 'When are you coming?' I asked, looking at Ann who in turn was looking at me, mystified.

'I will make the arrangements and let you know. Could you forward me a list of hotels in your area? It will only be three nights, a long weekend, as you say.'

'Why don't you stay with us?' I replied as Ann slowly disappeared under the sofa.

'No, I couldn't do that,' answered Miriam.

'Yes you can,' I said. 'We have a spare room. I insist.'

'Thank you, I would love to,' came the reply. We ended the call.

‘Why did you say that?’ asked Ann.

‘Ask what?’ I said.

‘Come stay with us,’ she retorted.

‘It’s only for three nights,’ I answered.

I received an email a few days later from Miriam.

Hi, Lee

I have organised my flight for Friday the 20th with British Airways, Hamburg to Heathrow leaving 16.45 and arriving at Heathrow 17.25 flight no ba960 and returning Heathrow 09.35 to Hamburg 10.20 on the 23rd. Hope this is OK with you.

That’s fine, I replied. *I will meet you at the arrival hall.*

That won’t be necessary, as I can book a cab to your house.

I will meet you, I replied.

You’re very kind, came the answer.

We finished emailing.

‘When is she coming?’ asked Ann.

‘The 20th,’ I said.

‘That gives us two weeks to get this place straight.’

‘What’s wrong with it?’ I said.

‘Look at that spare room, nobody’s slept in it since your mum. It needs decorating.’ Said Ann

Oh shit, I thought, *me and my mouth.*

On Thursday the 19th I phoned Miriam to see if everything was OK and she was still coming.

‘I am so looking forward to it,’ Miriam answered.

‘Great,’ I said. ‘Look forward to actually meeting you.’

‘I will have a card up with your name on it,’ I said, ‘so look out for me.’

‘I will see you tomorrow,’ answered Miriam.

We, that’s Ann and myself, got to Heathrow airport at approximately 16.40 and grabbed a coffee.

‘We are early,’ said Ann.

‘Yes, best be early than late,’ I joked.

It was 17.29 when the flight number flashed up on the monitor.

‘She’s landed,’ I said to Ann.

‘Why? Can you see her broom?’ she replied, laughing.

‘Hope you’re going to be civil,’ I said, smiling at her.

We waited in the hall, standing with my card and looking very silly, as the passengers emerged into the arrival hall.

‘I think that’s her,’ said Ann, as a very tall lady well-groomed in her sixties, maybe seventies, very slim, long blonde hair wearing a hat that resembled a dart board with arrows sticking out of it, and a smile longer than the airport.

‘Lee,’ she said, kissing me on the cheek as if we were old friends, ‘and you must be Ann,’ kissing her on the cheek. ‘It’s good to see you both,’ she said.

‘Good to meet you as well I said, at long last,’, taking her bag we left for the car park.

‘Good flight?’ said Ann.

‘Yes,’ she replied.

We arrived home. After removing her coat and that hat we had a cup of tea and a chat about Anna and Konrad.

‘Your English is quite exceptional,’ I said.

‘Yes, I was made to learn it when I was a little girl. Anna could speak English very well too I believe,’ said Miriam.

After our little chat, Ann took her on a tour of the house. I took her bag to her room.

‘My room looks lovely,’ said Miriam to me as I was sitting down watching the TV. ‘It looks like it has just been decorated.’

Don’t even go there, I thought. ‘Thank you,’ I said.

On Saturday morning we took Miriam to St Mary’s.

‘What a beautiful church,’ she acclaimed. ‘Outstanding.’

We walked through the archway into the grounds and up to the front of the church.

I said, ‘The graves are at the back there next to the tree,’ to Miriam.

‘Oh,’ she said, looking very pale with a painful look on her face.

'Are you OK?' asked Ann sympathetically.

'Yes, I am fine,' said Miriam as we walked down the side of the church towards the graves. It sounds strange but as we got closer to the graves it got more quieter and more peaceful;. We stood at the foot of the graves just staring, not saying a word. As I looked at Miriam I could see her mumbling quietly under her breath, then a tear ran down her cheek as she studded the inscriptions on the headstones. I nudged Ann and we backed off, returning to the car, leaving Miriam with her thoughts and to grieve alone.

It was about half an hour later when Miriam returned to the car, wiping the tears away from her eyes.

'Are you OK?' asked Ann, cuddling her.

'Yes, I'm fine,' she replied.

'Thank you,' she said. 'I needed to see them.'

'I know,' said Ann, as she took her by the hand and sat her back in the car.

That night after dinner we sat around the table and talked about Anna, Konrad and Katarina again.

'They must have been desperate to get away,' I said.

'They were,' said Miriam. 'According to my mother they were so in love. I meant to bring you some photos of Konrad and Anna's wedding but I forgot. I have a lovely one of Katrina which I will send you.'

'That would be lovely,' said Ann, and I agreed. We sat and talked for hours.

'Right,' I said, 'I am going to check the kids then I am going to bed.'

'Yes, I will retire as well,' said Miriam. 'Good night, and thank you again,' she said as she drifted upstairs.

On Sunday we took her on a walking tour of Rochford and drove around the surrounding areas. She saw the site where Konrad had worked as a baker, which was now a block of offices.

'It is such a wonderful town,' she exclaimed. 'You must come to Hamburg.'

'We would love to,' replied Ann.

'That's it,' said Miriam, 'we must make a date.'

We returned home.

Ann asked, 'What would you like for tea?'

'Why don't we all go to the pub for dinner?' suggested Miriam. 'My, how do you say, treat. You would like that children?'

'Yes please,' answered Leanne.

'I can't expect you to pay, you're our guest,' I said.

'Don't be silly, it's my thank you to you,' said Miriam.

'Oh, if you insist,' I said. 'I'll change my shirt.' As I ran up the stairs.

'Lee!' shouted Ann. 'Sorry about that, Miriam, he is rude.'

Miriam laughed.

That night we turned in Miriam went to bed about 10 pm, Ann followed about 10.30pm and I retired about midnight. As I climbed the stairs I could hear Miriam snoring.

'Wow,' I chuckled to myself, 'I bet she doesn't know she's that loud.'

As I passed her door it opened suddenly, very slowly. As I stared into the room I could see a black figure leaning over Miriam, seemingly stroking her hair. As I stood rooted to the spot it lifted its head and body then turned towards me.

It has to be Anna, I thought., Anna lifted her right arm then stretched it out , pointing her burnt finger at me , as I looked at her, I felt the cold presence of something or someone passing me it was the little girl Katarina, she run up to Anna and held on to her hand , They both stood there for a few moments looking at me before they faded away. I closed the door and went to bed.

The next morning we were all up at 06.00, had our breakfast and left for Heathrow. We arrived on time.

'Goodbye,' said Mariam. 'I have had a wonderful time. You will come to Hamburg.'

'Yes, yes we will,' I replied. 'Maybe next year.'

'Goodbye, Leanne,' she said, giving her a kiss and a cuddle while placing an envelope in her coat pocket when she was not looking. Then turning to Anthony and doing the same, to his disgust.

'Keep in touch,' said Ann, kissing her on the cheek.

'I will,' she replied, 'and Lee, I could never thank you enough.'

'It's my pleasure,' I said. 'You had better go, that's your call.'

With that she cuddled me and kissed my cheek, turned and headed through departures.

As we were about to drive out of the airport Leanne said, 'What's this?' as she retrieved the envelope from her coat pocket.

'I have one as well,' said Anthony.

'Well, open them then, kids,' I said, turning to them.

'What have you got?' said Ann, turning to them as well.

'Wow, look,' they said, holding up the cross and chains that started this whole story.

It's been 12 years now. Ann and myself still live at Cedar Cottage. Anthony got married to a girl called Lisa; they have 3 children, Lily who is 5, Charlie, 3, and Sophie who is 1. They moved into a 3 bedroom flat situated over a shop that sells mobile phones that they own. Yes, my son is an entrepreneur.

Leanne went to college and then went on to university where she studied accountancy. She got a high-flying job with a firm of accountants in Cambridge. She looks after Anthony's books as well, which is handy. She moved into a flat, as well with her partner, Gemma. Ummm, I don't think Horst would have approved. I'm sure of that.

Both kids still have the cross and chains Miriam gave them. Anthony's resides in Lisa's jewellery box. Leanne never takes hers off. As for Glen, he's got a bird. Might go somewhere, might not. His words, not mine.

Sadly, Jack died in October 2016. He nearly made it to one hundred, bless him. He was the only child of John and Martha. He was married in 1959 to a lovely lady called Jennifer, who sadly couldn't have children and died of the big c in 1988. We stayed close to Jack and made sure he was OK. Before Jack died, he gave me that clock which now sits proudly on my sideboard. We don't know what happened about his house' it stayed empty for about two years before a removal lorry arrived to take away the furniture. I remember going out and asking the driver what was happening to the house. His reply was it was going to auction.

It was about six months later another removal van arrived along with the new owner's, a young couple called Andrew and Annette. They had three children, Christopher 6, Gary 4, and 1 year old Brenda. Ann and Annette would do morning coffee and, to be honest, it was nice to see them and hear a baby crying. Brought back some memories of my two, but it was much nicer when they went through the front door back to their own house.

We received the framed photographs of Konrad and Anna's wedding day, and Katarina, from Miriam (she was right, Katrina was certainly a beautiful little girl), both photo's now proudly adorn our living room wall.

'Who's that?' asked Charlie one day. I said they were the people who lived here before us many many years ago. 'Where are they now?' he asked.

'In heaven,' I said.

'Why?' he asked.

'Because they were in the wrong place at the wrong time,' I said, expecting him to understand that remark.

We still keep in contact with Miriam and are planning another trip to Germany, this time to celebrate her 80th birthday next year. Should be emotional. I often think of the Beckers. I hoped deep down it was an accident and those heinous people who were in that mob showed remorse and sadness when the Beckers died. I suppose some people would understandably be full of hatred at losing a child, especially in the circumstances that those young lads died, but the Beckers had done nothing wrong. They paid with their lives, for being German. There's a new plaque on the memorial wall for those brave lads that died during that odious war, donated by the parish council. According to Jack, of the five boys that came of age seventeen that year, one was killed in action, two sustained wounds and returned home to a hero's welcome and two missed the war as their birthdays were in December and the war had finally ended on 11th November 1918. They still had to go to France; thankfully, they came back safe and well.

There have been no more apparitions or supernatural incidents since we gave back the crosses and chains to Miriam, only for her to give back to Anthony and Leanne.

I hope Konrad found Anna and Katrina and can rest in peace. We still tend to their graves. We left some flowers there only the other day. All my research and discoveries were all due to the internet (and I must admit, some luck, such as the German guy in Ipswich). It's a wonderful, amazing thing the internet, when used properly. I would have had to have spent hours, if not days, trouncing around the globe looking for answers and would have probably given up but it's been a remarkable journey which I would encourage other people to do.

Finally, the ship that the Beckers sailed on, the SS Kaiser Wilhelm der Grosse, was converted to an armed merchant cruiser and was sunk by H.M.S highflyer in 1914 and we heard that Father Patrick left the priesthood and is now working as a cashier at an Esso service station just outside Belfast. We still don't know what happened that day. As for me I am now retired, to Ann's disgust, but then she has always been retired, if you can call bringing up two kids a job. I would never say that to her face though, lol.

The End

Biography

I was born on Bancroft Rd, Stepney, East London on the 14th of May 1956. At the age of 3 my family moved to Dagenham in Essex. I left Gilbert Miles Comprehensive School at 15 in 1971 and had various jobs. It was at one of my jobs (Bartons of Kemp Rd Dagenham) I met my wife Pam in 1977. We were married in 1981 and have 2 children, Lee and Stacey. We now live in Girvan, South Ayrshire, Scotland. This is the first book I have written (hopefully not my last). Hope you enjoy it.

Thank you

www.ingramcontent.com/pod-product-compliance
Ingram Content Group UK Ltd.
Pitfield, Milton Keynes, MK11 3LW, UK
UKHW040013200726
13854UKWH00001B/183